Gooey Goblins

Candy Fairies

Halloween Special

Gooey Goblins

HELEN PERELMAN

ILLUSTRATED BY

ERICA-JANE WATERS

ALADDIN
NEW YORK   LONDON   TORONTO   SYDNEY

ALADDIN

An imprint of Simon & Schuster Children's Publishing Division

1230 Avenue of the Americas, New York, NY 10020

First Aladdin paperback edition August 2011

Text copyright © 2011 by Helen Perelman Bernstein

Illustrations copyright © 2011 by Erica-Jane Waters

All rights reserved, including the right of reproduction in whole or in part in any form.

ALADDIN is a trademark of Simon & Schuster, Inc., and related logo is a registered trademark of Simon & Schuster, Inc.

For information about special discounts for bulk purchases, please contact Simon & Schuster Special Sales at 1-866-506-1949 or business@simonandschuster.com.

The Simon & Schuster Speakers Bureau can bring authors to your live event.

For more information or to book an event contact the Simon & Schuster Speakers Bureau at 1-866-248-3049 or visit our website at www.simonspeakers.com.

Designed by Karin Paprocki

The text of this book was set in Berthold Baskerville Book.

Manufactured in the United States of America 0711 OFF

2 4 6 8 10 9 7 5 3 1

Library of Congress Control Number 2011924976

ISBN 978-1-4424-2213-1

ISBN 978-1-4424-2214-8 (eBook)

For Ben Spector, who is spook-tacular!

Contents

Contents

Gooey Goblins

CHAPTER

1

Melted Mess

Cocoa the Chocolate Fairy, Melli the Caramel Fairy, and Berry the Fruit Fairy soared over Chocolate River. A cool autumn breeze ruffled their wings, but they stayed their course. Nothing was going to stop them from heading to the far end of Gummy Forest.

 1

"Look, there's Dash!" Cocoa called. As the three fairy friends neared Peppermint Grove, they saw their tiny friend Dash shooting up to meet them.

"You are right on time," Dash said as she flew alongside her friends. She looked at Berry and smiled. "This must be important. You are never on time!"

Berry shot Dash a sour look. "The sugar fly said Raina's message was urgent. I can be on time when I need to be!"

"And yet she still had time to put on her best sugar-jewel necklace," Cocoa added with a sly grin.

"Just because I was rushing doesn't mean I have to look sloppy," Berry replied. Berry always liked to look her best and was usually sporting a new piece of jewelry that she had made herself from sparkling sugarcoated fruit chews.

"What do you think this is all about?" Melli asked. She was worried about her friend Raina the Gummy Fairy. Usually Raina didn't overreact to situations. She was very calm and always followed the rules.

"Maybe she just couldn't find something in the Fairy Code Book and needs our help," Cocoa joked.

"No, there's definitely something strange blowing around the valley," Dash said. She looked back at her friends. "And no, it's not just the cold autumn wind," she added.

Melli had to agree with Dash. "This is the busiest time in Sugar Valley, and we shouldn't be distracted from our work. Candy Corn Fields is already full of tall stalks."

The four fairies flew in silence for a moment. Then they saw the tops of the gummy trees.

"I can't wait to see Raina," Melli said. "I hope she's all right."

"We just saw her yesterday," Berry told her. "Don't be so dramatic. I'm sure she's fine."

Cocoa flew ahead, and then called back over her shoulder, "I don't think it's Raina we need to be concerned about." She pointed to the south end of the forest. "Look at those trees!"

The four friends gasped as they saw the melted leaves of the gummy trees. Normally, the branches were filled with bright rainbow gummy fruits.

"No wonder she called us," Berry whispered.

"Let's go find her," Dash said.

The fairies flew deeper into the forest. There were puddles everywhere from the melted gummy candies.

"I never thought I would say this," Dash said, "but Gummy Forest is a melted mess!" She flew over a rainbow puddle. Even though Dash was the smallest of all the Candy Fairies, she was always hungry and was the most adventurous eater. If the melted gummies didn't appeal even to Dash, the fairies knew things were *really* bad.

"Sweet sugar!" Raina shouted when she saw her friends. "I'm so glad you got here!"

"Oh, Raina," Melli called, rushing down to give her friend a hug. "What happened here?"

"I'm not really sure," Raina said, her voice full

of concern. "When I woke up this morning, the forest looked . . . melted!"

Cocoa, Berry, and Dash landed beside her. Their faces told Raina all she needed to know.

"It still looks awful here, doesn't it?" the Gummy Fairy asked. "The poor forest animals don't know what to make of all this. I tried my best to take away some of the melted candies and clean up some of the puddles, but that doesn't seem to be making a difference. The forest is still a mess."

"Are you okay?" Cocoa asked. She put her arm around Raina.

Raina sat down on a melted log on the ground. "I'm fine," she said with a heavy sigh. "I've been doing all sorts of research. And nothing seems to match up. All I know is that the forest animals and gummy candies are all in danger."

"It's definitely eerie, not cheery, here," Berry mumbled. "Are you sure this isn't some kind of spooky trick by Mogu?"

Raina shook her head. "I don't think so. This is really bad. Even for a tricky troll."

"I wouldn't put anything past Mogu," Cocoa said. "That old salty troll is sour."

"Yes," Raina agreed, "but Mogu loves gummy candy. I can't see him wanting to ruin it."

The fairies all knew that Mogu lived in Black Licorice Swamp and that he and his Chuchies often came to swipe candy from Gummy Forest. The troll and his round little workers loved candy too much to spoil the crops.

Berry looked closely at the melted trees. "I think you're right. These candies are ruined . . . even for a troll to eat."

"I told you something was going on," Dash mumbled.

Standing with her hands on her hips, Berry shook her head. "You're not saying what I think you're saying, are you?" She smiled at Dash. "You've been reading too many Caramel Moon stories."

"Most of those stories are based on truth," Dash said. She loved to read all the spooky tales that fairies had spun about the full moon in the tenth month of the year. "Those aren't just ghost stories." Dash looked over at Melli and Raina. "Tell them!"

"Well, some of those stories are just meant to

entertain," Raina said. "But others are based on true occurrences."

Dash gloated for a minute, but then a melted candy snapped off its vine and fell on her head. She rubbed her forehead and looked to Raina. "What do you think this is all about?"

Raina plucked a droopy gummy branch off a tree. "Has anyone else seen anything strange going on in Sugar Valley?" She glanced over at Dash. "Or heard anything strange?"

"The gummy flowers over by Chocolate River did look melted," Cocoa told Raina.

Dash's silver wings flapped nervously as she spoke. "Last night I heard howling and moaning in Peppermint Grove," she whispered.

"Something isn't right in Sugar Valley," Melli muttered. "Oh, and there's so much to do! Think of all the fall candy crops that could be ruined."

"Let's not get our wings dipped in syrup yet," Berry told her friends. "We can get to the bottom of this."

A sugar fly appeared and dropped a note for Raina. She read the letter quickly and then showed her friends. "The note is from Candy Castle. Princess Lolli is calling a meeting of all the fairies. We are supposed to go to the Royal Gardens at Candy Castle now."

Melli gasped, and her hand flew up to her mouth.

"If Princess Lolli is calling us to the castle, the situation has to be sour!" Dash exclaimed.

"Not necessarily," Cocoa said, trying to keep her friends calm. But in her heart she wasn't so sure. Princess Lolli was the kind and gentle

 10

ruler of all of Sugar Valley. She didn't often call a meeting of all the fairies—unless something was *very* urgent.

The fairies flew off to Candy Castle hoping that all would soon be right in Sugar Valley.

CHAPTER 2

Candy Castle Surprise

There was a noisy crowd at the sugar gates of Candy Castle. Fairies from all over Sugar Valley were waiting patiently to enter the Royal Gardens. Princess Lolli's throne made of peppermint sticks, colorful fruit leather, and sugarcoated jewels sat in the middle of the gardens on a large square platform. The Royal

Fairy Guards were busy trying to keep all the fairies calm and quiet as the gates were opened. Raina led her friends to the stage. If there was an announcement, Raina wanted to be front and center to hear every word.

Berry checked out the scene. "Looks like everyone in Sugar Valley is here today," she said. She noticed that even the fairies from Sour Orchard were there. Those fairies had to travel the farthest and didn't always come to Candy Castle gatherings.

"This must be big news if even the Sour Orchard Fairies are here," Raina whispered.

"Look, there's Lemona," Berry said. Lemona had been a big help to Berry when Berry had picked wild candy hearts along Chocolate River and didn't know that the candies had unexpected magical powers. Berry and Raina had traveled to Sour Orchard to meet her.

"Berry!" Lemona called when she saw the Fruit Fairy. The elderly Sour Orchard Fairy flew up to Berry and her friends. "This is quite a gathering, isn't it?" she said. "I haven't seen this many fairies together since the ice storm years ago."

"I think everyone in Sugar Valley is here," Berry replied.

Lemona leaned closer. "I heard from someone that even Mogu is here!"

"Mogu!" Cocoa exclaimed, overhearing the big news. "Why would that salty old troll be here?"

Melli shuddered. Just thinking about the greedy troll made her nervous. "Why would

Princess Lolli invite him here?" she wondered out loud.

"Maybe she didn't invite him," Dash said, glancing around. "I'm telling you, there is definitely something spooky going on."

A cold chill fluttered their wings, and the fairies all huddled together as they waited for the meeting to begin. The caramel trumpets blared and the castle doors opened. Princess Lolli flew to her throne with her four top Royal Fairy advisers. Raina recognized Tula, a kind old fairy who had been very nice to her during Candy Fair. Candy Fair was held every four years at Candy Castle and was the biggest event for showing new candy. She noticed right away that all the Royal Fairies had serious expressions on their faces.

"Boiling hot chocolate!" Cocoa blurted out.

She couldn't say anything more. All she could do was point at the castle doors. There, ambling slowly out the door, was Mogu!

"Lemon drops!" Raina gasped. "A troll in the Royal Gardens? This really is a big deal."

The fairies watched as the white-haired troll waddled through the crowd. His clothes were tattered and stained with chocolate. He kept his eyes straight ahead as he walked with four Chuchies chasing after him. The Chuchies tried to keep up on their thin, short legs, but Mogu walked ahead. They jabbered quietly to one another as they made their way to the princess's throne.

"This is so *not* mint," Dash grumbled.

"Shhh," Melli said, trying to hear what the princess was saying. "The meeting is starting."

A great hush spread through the crowd as Mogu and the four Chuchies stood around the throne.

"You could hear a gumdrop fall here now," Raina whispered to Berry.

Princess Lolli stood up. "Welcome, everyone. And thank you for coming. I know this meeting comes at a very busy time for all of you." She took a moment and looked around at the crowd. "I'm sure you are all wondering about our guests." She waved her hand to her right, where Mogu and the Chuchies were standing. "They have some news to share with us."

Mogu stepped forward. "There are goblins haunting Sugar Cove. They are melting the candy and making a mess." The troll smacked his lips together loudly. "I've seen a trail heading out

 18

past Gummy Forest to the sea. I'm sure those goblins are in Sugar Cove, across the Vanilla Sea. Nothing a goblin likes better than melted candy."

All the fairies gasped as they took in this information.

"We have to do something!" Mogu ranted. "These pesky goblins want to melt down Sugar Valley! They must be stopped."

"Why doesn't he do something?" Berry said, glaring at the troll. Her arms were crossed tightly across her chest.

There was talking and sighing heard throughout the gardens. Princess Lolli held up her hands to quiet the crowd. "I know this is very upsetting, but the fact is that there are a few areas of Sugar Valley that are in danger. There have been reports of melted candy."

"It's not just Gummy Forest?" Raina said, sinking down to the ground. She put her head in her hands. "This is worse than I thought."

"We're supposed to believe Mogu?" Melli asked. "This is a little hard to swallow."

"For once I think that salty old troll is right!" Dash said.

"At a time like this," Princess Lolli said to the crowd, "we must all work together." She noticed the worried looks on many of the faces. "I am not convinced that there really are goblins. But I am sure that we need to investigate these meltings."

"Why would goblins want to melt Gummy Forest?" a tall Gummy Fairy called out.

"And melt sugar around Sugar Valley?" a young Fruit Fairy asked.

"Goblins are mischievous," Cocoa suggested.

"I cannot deny that there is some trickery going on," Princess Lolli explained. "And since the fall crops are so precious, I decree that a team of fairies will journey to Sugar Cove to explore."

Many of the fairies started to talk. Sugar Cove was a long journey from Candy Kingdom. A fairy would need to be very brave and sail across the sea to make the trip. Princess Lolli quieted the crowd once again.

"Please take a moment and decide if you are up for the journey," the princess told the fairies. "I will be in the castle awaiting the right team for the task."

Raina looked at her friends. They all nodded. They wanted to go!

CHAPTER 3

A Sweet Team

The Sugar Valley fairies were buzzing about the news of goblins and about who would go to Sugar Cove. Raina overheard many conversations as she flew over to a corner of the garden where her friends had gathered to talk.

"Oh, we have to go!" Cocoa said. She pumped

her hand up in the air. "We are just the fairy team for the quest. We can do this!"

Melli's hazel eyes grew wide. "I don't know, Cocoa," she said. "Even Mogu looked afraid. And he's a troll!"

"I guess trolls get scared too," Dash said quietly.

"What do you think, Raina?" Berry asked.

Raina studied her friends for a moment. "I know everyone here is excited and wants to find an answer. But I really don't think this is a goblin hunt."

Dash sat down on the ground and pulled a mint stick out of her bag. "Well, that's good to hear," she mumbled.

Melli rolled her eyes. "Oh, Dash, how can you eat at a time like this?" She knew Dash had a big appetite for such a tiny fairy, but this didn't seem like the time to snack.

"When I'm nervous, I eat," Dash replied, smiling. "And come to think of it, there's really no time I don't like to eat!"

Cocoa and Berry laughed, and Melli rolled her eyes again.

Raina clapped her hands. "We have to focus," she said. "I know Melli and Dash are nervous, but I don't believe this is about goblins."

"You think Mogu is lying?" Melli asked.

"When have you ever trusted a troll?" Berry asked.

Cocoa looked toward the castle. "Maybe this time we have to," she said. "We all saw Gummy Forest. If Black Licorice Swamp is in the same shape, all of Sugar Valley is in danger."

"And during fall harvest!" Melli blurted out. "Think of all that candy. . . ."

"I am!" Dash said, springing up. "We have to do something. What if Mogu is right and there are goblins trying to ruin Sugar Valley candy?"

Raina paced back and forth between the gumdrop trees. "Remember when we made a ghost out of Berry's shawl and the Chuchies believed that there was a ghost in Candy Corn Fields?"

"Sweet caramel, I sure do," Melli said. She had been so proud of her friends for solving that mystery—and for saving the candy corn crop.

Fluttering her wings, Raina flew up in the air. "So maybe Mogu and the Chuchies *believe* that there are goblins, but there really aren't any?" She stopped and tapped her finger on her chin.

"If it's not goblins, what could it be?" Berry asked.

"Princess Lolli didn't say if she believed Mogu or not," Raina continued. "If she were certain, she wouldn't be sending a team out to explore." Raina flew into the center of the circle her friends had formed. "Don't you all want to be part of this?"

"I'm in," Dash blurted out. She was always up for an adventure, and if this one involved saving the candy in Sugar Valley, she was up for the journey.

"Count me in too," Berry said. "I'm not afraid of a troll *or* goblins."

Raina looked over at Cocoa and Melli. "What do you think?" she asked.

Cocoa nodded. "I'll go," she said. "I'm not

sure I believe Mogu, but after seeing Gummy Forest this morning, I know I have to do something."

All eyes were on Melli. "Okay," she said reluctantly. "I'll go. Friends stick together."

"Sure as sugar," Raina said, smiling.

Raina hoped Princess Lolli would pick them to take this journey. She had to—they were the prefect fairy team for the task.

Dash quickly noticed that no one else was in the throne room when they arrived. "Where is everyone?" she whispered to Berry.

Berry spun around. "I guess we're the only ones who want to go," she said hesitantly.

As the friends approached the throne, Mogu stepped forward.

"These are the only fairies you've got?" Mogu

28

bellowed. "These little fairies are going to be no match for the goblins in Sugar Cove. Why, they are no match for anyone. *Baaaaaah-haaaaa!*"

"Princess Lolli," Raina said, ignoring Mogu, "we'd like to go to Sugar Cove and find out what is happening. We are a special group of fairies and have different candy strengths to battle whatever comes our way." She looked over at Mogu. "And it's not just about size or age."

Smiling, Princess Lolli nodded. "You are very wise, Raina," she said. "And I am proud of you five fairies for stepping forward to help in Candy Kingdom's time of need." She got up from her throne and leaned in close to the fairies. "Are you sure you are up to the trip? Sugar Cove is very far from here."

The five fairies flapped their wings quickly.

"We've talked this over, and sure as sugar we all want to go," Berry stated.

"Salty sours," Mogu grumbled, hitting his hand on his knee. "One fiery look from those goblins, and these fairies will be deep-fried."

"Mogu," Princess Lolli said gently, "I said that I would handle this, and I will. So kindly refrain from saying anything bitter in my castle." She winked at the fairies in front of her. "We all appreciate your dedication," she told them.

Raina glanced at her friends. She hoped they were all feeling as proud as she was at that moment. They were the team that was going to save Candy Kingdom from being a melted sugar wasteland.

CHAPTER 4

Royal Sugar

*B*aaaaaah-haaaaaa!" Mogu laughed. His
laughter echoed in the royal throne room and
sent shivers to the tips of
the fairies' wings. "You
can't be serious, can you?"
He leaped out of his seat and
walked over to the fairies. "No

one else is coming forward to go to Sugar Cove except these little fairies?" He licked his lips. "They might make tasty candy, but can they scare a goblin?"

Cocoa lunged forward. She had dealt with Mogu before, and she was ready to answer him. She felt Melli's hand on her arm and looked back at her friend. Melli was pointing toward Princess Lolli. The princess was looking right at Cocoa, motioning for her to wait.

Feeling her anger bubble up inside of her, Cocoa bit her lip. How could she not say anything? She had tricked the salty troll before, and she would prove him wrong again.

"Mogu," Princess Lolli said sweetly. She walked over and stood beside him. "You came to me with this problem. And I appreciate your

 33

efforts to keep the candy in the kingdom safe and delicious." She stopped and watched as Mogu grinned. Some of his teeth were missing, and his smile was a bit crooked. "I would like to handle this my way," the sweet princess continued. "And I believe this team of fairies offers the right blend of ingredients to solve this mystery."

Cocoa smiled at the princess and bowed her head. Though it was hard for her to hold her tongue, Cocoa knew that Princess Lolli was right. Fighting with Mogu now would not solve anything. Everyone in the kingdom had to work together. She wasn't sure if there were goblins or not, but she had seen the melted candy and wanted to stop that from happening again.

"Princess Lolli," Raina said, "we're honored that you think we can do this."

 34

The princess smiled. She pushed her jeweled tiara up on her strawberry-blond hair. "I think you will get to the bottom of this mystery," she said, "and save us all."

"Sure as sugar!" Dash exclaimed.

"Wait here for a moment," Princess Lolli said. "I want to give you something for the journey." She went out the side door of the room and returned with a small basket made of rainbow licorice strands. "Please take this with you," she said.

Dash peeked inside the basket. "But there's nothing in the basket!" she exclaimed.

The princess giggled. "We are going to put things inside right now, Dash," she explained. "I want each of you to put one of your own candies in the basket. You may use the royal sugar in the golden bucket." She pointed to the large bucket by her throne, which was filled with the finest sugar in all of Sugar Valley.

If a fairy stuck her hand in the sugar bucket, she would pull out a piece of her own special candy. Royal sugar was the basic ingredient of all Sugar Valley candy. When a fairy touched the fine sugar, she formed her own candy in her hand.

Cocoa and Melli went first and made a chocolate bar and a caramel square. Next Dash and Raina stepped up and pulled out a sparkling red-and-white mint and a rainbow gumdrop. Berry was last and took her time creating a bright red fruit-chew heart.

"I wish I could do that," Mogu moaned. "I'm hungry."

The Chuchies by his side jumped up and down on their thin legs. "Meeeeeee, meeee!" they squealed.

Tula handed Mogu and each of the Chuchies a sack of candy. "Thank you again for coming to us for help," she said. She pushed her sparkly glasses farther up on her nose. "And thank you for letting us handle the situation our way."

"Happy to help," Mogu said, grabbing the candy. "And always happy to eat!" He opened the bag and emptied the candy in his mouth. "I was hoping for that royal sack of candy." He spoke with his mouth open and showed off his black teeth. "Good luck out there in Sugar Cove,"

37

he said. He reached into his pocket and threw a black licorice rope into the candy basket. "Never know when you'll need some black licorice!"

With another loud laugh, he waddled out of the throne room with the Chuchies close behind.

Berry shook her head. "I'm glad he's gone," she said.

"Well, he did give us information," Raina told her. "We wouldn't have known there was anything unusual in Sugar Cove if Mogu hadn't come here."

"Raina is right," Princess Lolli said. "And I am so thankful that you five fairies will go exploring. Here is the map of the area," she told them. She handed Raina a scroll. "I want you to promise to send a sugar fly the moment you find yourselves in any danger."

"Thank you, princess," Melli said. Knowing that Princess Lolli would come if they were in need of help eased her mind.

"It's too dangerous to fly over the sea because the winds are strong and the fog is very heavy," Princess Lolli told the fairies. "Tula has arranged for a boat for you at the shores of Gummy Forest for your trip."

Raina took the map. "We will keep our eyes open," she told the princess.

"Be safe in your travels and think wisely before making any judgments or taking actions," Princess Lolli said.

"Be sure to stick together," Tula advised.

"Sure as sugar, we will," the five fairies said at the same time.

CHAPTER

5

Fairy Tales

Hot chocolate!" Cocoa exclaimed as the friends flew through the royal gates. "Did you see the look on Mogu's face? I can't wait to solve this mystery. We'll show that old troll."

"You can bet your chocolate-covered chips," Berry said, grinning. "He is so salty." She grimaced and shook her head.

"Seeing him in Candy Castle was strange," Raina added. "That seemed so wrong. Candy Castle is the sweetest place."

"That's for sure," Cocoa said. "But Princess Lolli knows just how to handle Mogu."

"Did you see how he gobbled up those candies Princess Lolli gave him?" Dash added. "And those Chuchies weren't much better."

"Come on, it's almost Sun Dip," Berry said. She was anxious to change the subject. "Let's go over to Red Licorice Lake."

The five friends left Candy Castle and flew toward the red sugar sands of Red Licorice Lake. Each day at Sun Dip the fairies met there to share a snack and talk about their day.

As the fairies flew the bright sun hit the top of the Frosted Mountains. The autumn sunset

was full of red, orange, and purple and looked deliciously inviting. The fairies all sat down, exhausted from their meeting with Princess Lolli.

"I still can't believe she's letting us go," Raina said. She took out the scroll the princess had given them and unrolled the map.

Melli came and sat down next to her, peering over her shoulder.

"Do you have any caramel sticks?" Dash asked her. When Melli didn't answer, the fairies all looked at her. They all realized at the same time that Melli hadn't said a word since they left Candy Castle.

"Are you all right?" Cocoa asked.

Melli looked around at her friends. "Did you notice that no other fairies wanted to go on this journey?"

Her friends all stared at her. They were well aware of that fact.

"No one else volunteered," Melli said. "And I know why no one else raised a wing to find who or what has been bewitching Sugar Cove," she added softly.

Her friends grew quiet.

"Do you remember who lives in the Vanilla

 45

Sea?" She pointed to the water on the map. "You have to cross the Vanilla Sea to get to Sugar Cove."

All the fairies stared blankly at Melli. Then Raina fluttered her wings. Raina loved books and knew the history of Candy Kingdom by heart. She had practically memorized the Fairy Code Book.

"You're thinking of Nillie, the sea serpent, aren't you?" Raina asked.

Dash flew up from her seat. "Who's that?"

"There are many spooky stories about Nillie," Berry said, waving her hand. "Those are just old stories fairies like to tell around full moons in the fields. Nillie is just a fairy tale."

"I remember hearing about Nillie!" Cocoa exclaimed. "She puts creatures under a sugar spell."

Cocoa, Melli, Dash, and Berry all looked to Raina. If anyone was going to know the answer, it was her.

Raina felt all their eyes on her. "Well . . . ," she said slowly. She looked up to the tall red stalks of licorice as she thought. "I always believed those tales were spun by fairies working in Sugar Cove. No one has really ever actually seen the serpent in the Vanilla Sea."

Brushing some sugar sand from her shoe, Berry sighed. "There are stories and there are facts," she said plainly. "We can't lose focus here. Even though other fairies are afraid of tall tales, we can't be. We need to get to the bottom of what is melting the candy."

Cocoa stood up. "Berry is right. There are so many candies ready for harvesting now. We need to make sure these goblins, or whatever they are, don't harm any more candy."

"I'm all for that," Dash said. "Bring on the scary and save the candy!"

Melli rolled up the scroll. "Sometimes stories are based on facts," she said. "And that is what I am afraid of."

"Let's think sweetly," Raina offered. "We should meet tomorrow at Gummy Forest dock."

"There is so much to do before we leave," Cocoa said. "How long do you think we'll be gone?"

"It doesn't take that long to sail the Vanilla Sea," Raina said thoughtfully. "We could probably be there tomorrow night."

"We're going to get there at night?" Melli asked. "That's not great timing."

"Oh, we'll be fine," Berry said. "Besides, we have the candy basket Princess Lolli gave us."

"Unless these are goblins who like to eat candy and not just melt it, we may need a little more than sweet luck," Dash said.

Melli wasn't too sure, and neither were any of her friends. But they had told the princess they would go, and now they had to stick to their promise.

CHAPTER

6

Setting Sail

In the morning clouds hung over the Frosted Mountains. Since the sun was blocked, the early daylight was dim and the air was chilly. The wind rustled the leaves on the caramel stalks outside Melli's window. As she packed for her trip to Sugar Cove, she shivered. Normally, she loved these fall mornings when all the other

fairies were sleeping and she could get to Candy Corn Fields to begin her work. She never minded if the sun was hiding behind a cloud or if the autumn winds were gusting. She loved fall harvest. There were so many delicious autumn caramel candies during this time. But today Melli was a little unsure about the journey to Sugar Cove. The thought of crossing the Vanilla Sea was making her wings shake!

Melli looked over at the sugar basket filled with candy. She knew that the kind princess would help if they needed her, yet this didn't calm her nerves.

Taking flight, she raced to Gummy Forest to meet her friends. The far side of the forest lined the shores of the Vanilla Sea and would be where they'd board the sailboat.

"Morning, Melli!" Raina called to her. The Gummy Fairy was already packing the boat with gear for the trip.

"Am I the first one here?" Melli asked.

"Nope," Cocoa chimed in. She popped up from the boat. "I got here a little while ago to help Raina with the boat."

Melli looked around. "No sign of Berry or Dash?" she asked.

A silver streak whizzed past Melli. "I'm here!" Dash squealed. She glanced down at the boat. "So mint!" she exclaimed. "I've never been on a sailboat before. And this one is pure sugar!" She inspected the creamy white boat with the rainbow fruit leather seats. "We're riding in style," she said, approving of the boat. "How fast does she go?"

53

Her friends all laughed. They knew Dash loved speed. She was one of the fastest fairies in the kingdom. Most of all she loved her sled, which she raced down the Frosted Mountains on at top speed. The faster the better for Dash!

"Too bad we're off to find goblins," Melli muttered, "not to win any races."

Dash was about to ask why Melli was all sticky and sour, but Berry interrupted her.

"Hello, fairies!" Berry cried from above. "I know, I'm late, but I am here!" She reached into her bag. "Check this compass out!" she said with a proud grin. "I found this at home. Isn't it supersweet?" She showed her friends the sugarcoated jewel compass. "This is going to lead us straight to Sugar Cove—even in the fog. We just need to sail west," she said, pointing to the bright pink *W* on the face of the compass.

"That is a *sugar-tastic* plan," Dash said.

"Did you add all the fruit jewels?" Raina asked. She leaned over to admire the bejeweled compass.

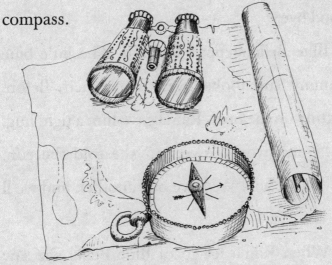

"Sure as sugar!" Berry said. "This compass is functional *and* fashionable."

Cocoa smiled. "*Choc-o-rific!* Leave it to Berry to come up with a fashion statement for any journey," she said.

"All aboard!" Raina cried.

As the friends got on the boat a few gummy bears and other gummy animals came out of the forest. They lined up along the shore to say good-bye.

Blue Belle stepped forward. The little blue gummy cub looked very concerned. Before getting on the boat, Raina gave him a tight hug.

"Don't worry, sweetie," she told the cub. "We'll be fine. We have one another, and we'll be safe."

When Raina let go of Blue Belle, she saw Princess Lolli standing on the dock. "I came to say good-bye too," she said. "And to thank you fairies again for taking this journey."

"We'll be careful," Raina assured her. "We

 56

have your basket with the candies and some other supplies."

"Send a sugar fly if anything happens, and I will be there at once," the princess reminded them.

A few of the forest animals helped push the boat out to sea, and the fairies all waved.

"We'll send word as soon as we see anything dangerous!" Raina called back to Princess Lolli. She sat at the back of the boat to steer with the rudder.

"Or even if we don't," Dash added. She looked at her friends and shrugged. "Sometimes those goblins are pretty sneaky!"

"Oh, Dash," Berry said. "Take hold of the ropes, and don't let go." She reached up to the boom of the sail. Melli sat with Raina at the stern of the boat.

Dash did as she was told, and the sail filled up with air, pushing the little boat farther out to the sea. Pretty soon the fairies could no longer see Gummy Forest.

"Keep watch for Rock Candy Isle," Raina said. She was hovering over the map. "That should be coming on our left."

"Yum." Dash sighed. "I love rock candy."

Melli gave Dash a sour look. "We are not stopping for a snack," she said. "I'd like to get to Sugar Cove before nighttime."

"The fog is very dense," Berry said. "I'm so glad we have this compass to guide us."

"Does that thing light up?" Melli asked.

"Arriving in the dark is going to be spooky." She gave herself a tight hug. "It's early in the morning, and we can't see a thing. Imagine what it'll be like at night!"

"We'll just go slow and stay the course," Raina said, looking at the map. "We should get there before the stars come out."

The sail above them began to ripple in the wind, and the boat swayed from side to side.

"What if Nillie doesn't like visitors?" Melli asked nervously. She looked out into the choppy sea. The breeze was gusting.

"I guess these are the winds Princess Lolli was talking about," Berry said. Her wings were being blown back, pushing her toward the back of the boat. "There's no way we could have flown in this."

"Um, or how about sail?" Dash asked. "I'm not feeling so well."

"Oh, Dash," Cocoa gasped. "Are you going to be seasick?"

Dash shook her head. "No, I'm okay," she said. She looked down at the bottom of the boat. "But I'm not feeling so good about the boat!" she shouted.

All the fairies followed Dash's finger. She was pointing to a corner of the boat, where water was coming in. The boat had a leak!

"Hot chocolate!" Cocoa screamed.

The water was rushing into the boat. The fairies had to do something—fast!

7

Sweet High Seas

"Melli, take the rudder," Raina instructed. "I know what to do."

Melli did as she was told, and she carefully switched places with Raina. She didn't take her eyes off Dash, who had her finger pressed on the hole.

"Hurry!" Dash exclaimed. The water was

seeping into the boat around Dash's small finger.

"Bittersweet," Cocoa said as she watched the water swirl around the bottom of the boat. "We have to do something!"

"Hold tight," Raina said. She looked inside the candy basket the princess had given them. "Ah, a sweet gumdrop." She fluttered her wings. "I knew that would come in handy," she said proudly. "I'll just plug up the hole." Raina stood back and admired her handiwork. "Leaky boat problem solved!"

All the fairies cheered. Raina smiled and took a bow. "I always loved sailing," she gloated. "I never fixed a boat with a gumdrop, but it is a handy thing to have aboard!"

The five friends settled into their seats as the water lapped around the boat.

Tugging on the ropes, Berry struggled to keep the sail full. The boom turned, and the sail soon filled out. "I think we're all right now. We should have smooth sailing from here."

"If we're lucky," Melli said glumly. She couldn't help but peer over the side of the boat. She was looking for signs of Nillie.

"No luck, just skill," Raina boasted, and winked at Berry. "We make a fine sailing team."

"Anytime!" Berry said happily. "I love sailing."

"I haven't seen Rock Candy Isle," Dash said. She squinted into the fog. "There's no way to see! It's like looking through a cloudy lens."

Raina checked the compass and the map. "We're still on course," she said. "We have to be patient."

Cocoa slid next to Melli. She had been watching her bite her nails. "Come on, Melli," she said, moving closer to her. "We're all together. Please don't be so nervous. We're safe here in the boat."

"This choppy sea makes me feel like Nillie might be near," the Caramel Fairy confessed. "A sea monster would not be happy to see us. And I don't want to upset her."

Why did Melli have to bring up the idea of Nillie? Cocoa thought. She tried to think of something to say to her friend, but she didn't get a chance. The boat started to rock again, and she had to move seats to hold the sail ropes.

Melli's face went white as sugar. "Oooooh!" she cried. She lunged forward to grip Cocoa's hand.

"Maybe it's the goblins," Dash said.

Berry shot Dash a sour look. "Dash!" she scolded. "Not helpful!"

Dash shrugged and stuck a caramel stick in her mouth. "I was just thinking out loud. Besides, you were all thinking the same thing."

From her bag Berry took out a pair of jeweled binoculars. "I knew these would come in handy," she said.

"Functional and fashionable, right?" Dash said as she saw Berry's decorated binoculars.

Berry didn't pay attention to Dash's comment. She was concentrating on the sight ahead. "Licking lollipops!" she exclaimed. "Even with these I can't see through the fog." She passed the binoculars to each of her friends.

"Wait!" Melli exclaimed. "I see something!"

In a brief clearing of the heavy fog, Melli saw Rock Candy Isle. The small island was filled with overgrown sticks of rock candy in a rainbow of colors. The hard candy looked liked jewels sparkling in the middle of the Vanilla Sea.

"Does anyone live there?" Cocoa asked as she peered through the lens for her turn.

"Lucky fairy!" Dash said, licking her lips when Cocoa passed the binoculars to her. She would love to taste the large chunks of rock candy.

Raina shook her head. "No one lives there," she said. "It's just a small island . . . with the best rock candy." She looked over at Dash. "And no, we're not stopping!"

After putting the binoculars away, Berry grabbed the sail ropes. "I don't think we could stop even if we wanted. This wind is really blowing hard." She struggled with the ropes as she let the sail out.

The sailboat was tossed, and a wave of water splashed into the boat. All the fairies were soaking wet.

"Sweet strawberries!" Berry cried. She wiped her eyes and wrung the bottom of her dress. "I wasn't planning on going for a swim!"

"Oooh!" Melli cried out again. She shook off the water and buried her head in her hands. "I don't like this. I was not meant for the high seas!"

"No wonder you never wanted to go sailing with us," Raina said to her Caramel Fairy friend. She glanced around the boat. "Everyone all right?"

When all the fairies responded that they were

fine, Raina sighed. She had known this journey would be challenging, but she'd had no idea the sea would be so rough. She just hoped they reached the cove before Sun Dip . . . and nighttime.

"Did you see that?" Cocoa gasped. She pointed to the water.

"Nillie?" Melli asked, uncovering one eye.

"No," Cocoa replied. "It looked like an animal. Maybe a turtle?"

"A caramel turtle?" Melli exclaimed, perking up. She peeled her fingers away from her eyes. "Sweet sugars, I've always wanted to see one. I've only seen pictures in a book."

The boom spun around and nearly hit Melli on the head as she leaned out of the boat.

"Careful!" Raina scolded.

69

"Maybe you can talk to them," Berry suggested. "I can see the cove. We aren't far. If the turtles stop hitting the boat, we'll get there faster."

Melli shook the water off her wings. She hesitated and looked back at her friends. They were watching as she kneeled down closer to the water. In a flash there was a bale of turtles peeking up at her. Their shells were a deep caramel color with beautiful patterns of swirling shapes etched into them. Melli's expression softened when she realized the turtles were just scared. They meant no harm, and with a loving touch from sweet Melli they were calm.

"Hot caramel," Melli said. "They are just scared." She glanced over at Dash. "Can you pass me the caramel chew from the royal basket?"

Dash reached into the basket and gave Melli the caramel. "This should keep those yapping turtles busy chewing," she said, smiling.

"Sure as sugar, you have a way with those turtles," Cocoa cooed as she watched Melli pull off pieces of the caramel to feed the hungry turtles. "Thank goodness, because I can barely hold on to these ropes anymore."

"Not much longer," Raina said. She was glad that Melli seemed to be a little more relaxed on the boat—and that the turtles were letting them pass.

"I see Sprinkle Sands Beach!" Dash said, flapping her wings excitedly. She was looking through Berry's binoculars. "*So mint!* The beach is beautiful. We're at Sugar Cove!"

CHAPTER 8

Candy Cliffs

As the sailboat moved toward Sprinkle Sands Beach, all five fairies drew their breath in. All around the cove were large candy rocks and colorful trees and vines. The setting sun cast an orange glow on the steep cliffs. None of the fairies had ever seen anything like it before.

"Those are the Candy Cliffs," Raina whispered, gazing up. "They are even more beautiful—and higher—than any picture I've ever seen."

"Hot chocolate," Cocoa said, her eyes wide. "Those are some big cliffs."

"This place is gorgeous!" Berry exclaimed.

As they stared up at the cliffs the fairies saw a few caves nestled in the rocks high up. They all had thoughts of goblins popping out at any moment, but Raina snapped everyone's attention back to the task at hand.

"We need to pull the boat up on the shore," she said. "If we all pull together, we should be able to get the boat out of the water."

The fairies all jumped out of the boat. The water in the cove was warm and calm, unlike out in the Vanilla Sea. Holding on to the rope, they each pulled the boat. The warm cove water lapped at their knees. The water was so clear that they could see down to the sugar sand bottom. As they moved closer to the shore, the water got shallower and it became harder to pull the boat along on the sand.

"Just a little more," Raina called to her friends. "We should move the boat away from the shoreline. We don't want to have it float out to sea."

"Then we'd be stranded here," Melli muttered, looking around. The setting sun was slowly sinking down. Nighttime would soon follow. The light was no longer orange, but a cool, dark purple. Melli's wings fluttered. *Nighttime is when goblins come out,* she thought.

Cocoa put her hand out and touched Melli's shoulder. She didn't like that Melli was worrying so much. "Dash, do you have any peppermints to light up?" She thought a little light would help her Caramel Fairy friend.

"I do," Dash said brightly. "There isn't much of a moon tonight." She squinted up to the darkening sky. There was only a tiny sliver of a moon peeking out of the evening sky.

Once Dash cracked the mint sticks, there was a minty glow that helped the fairies see. In the pale light the cove seemed a little spooky, but some light was better than no light.

"Maybe we should go exploring," Berry said. She looked up at the cliffs. "We could fly up there and check out those caves."

 76

"We can barely see," Melli replied. "Plus, there are too many rocks. Maybe we should wait till morning."

"Licking lollipops!" Berry cried. "This is why we are here. If there really are goblins, now would be the time to see them."

Cocoa glanced at Melli. She saw that she had lowered her head. Her purple wings sagged low to the ground, and she didn't say a word. Raina, Dash, and Berry all waited for her response. If they didn't all go together, they wouldn't go.

Finally Melli looked up from her sand-covered feet. "You're right," she said. "This is why we came. We should go now."

"You sure you'll be okay?" Cocoa asked.

"Yes," Melli answered. "Princess Lolli is

counting on us." She paused. "Actually, all of Sugar Valley is counting on us. I don't want to disappoint anyone."

"And we want to get to the bottom of this mystery," Raina added.

"We're just the fairies for the job," Berry boasted. "No troll is going to scare me with some goblin story. I want to find the *real* answer."

Raina smiled at her brave friend. "Well, the answer may be up there in the caves," she said.

"So let's go!" Dash cried. She led the way with a glowing peppermint light.

The five fairies flew up the steep cliff. Near the top Dash landed on a large rock that jutted out from the cliff. "I think we should walk from here," she said. "It's a little too dark to be flying."

"You're right," Raina said. "It's not safe to fly in the dark."

The fairies walked in single file, holding their mint sticks. There was complete silence as they explored. This was not the landscape they were used to in Sugar Valley.

"Ouch!" Berry cried. She fell down, holding her leg. "Sweet sours," she moaned. "I cut my leg on that rock!"

The fairies all gathered around her. Raina held her peppermint up to get a better look. "Oh, Berry, you have a deep cut," she said.

"I have something for that," Dash told her. "In the royal candy basket I have just the thing."

Berry looked over at the small fairy. "Are you sure that will work?"

Dash opened the mint candy and spread the

 80

white gel over Berry's wound. The cool gel helped soothe Berry's wound instantly. "A little bit of peppermint goes a long way," she said.

Smiling, Berry reached out to hug Dash. "I've never been so thankful for your mint. That stuff is amazing."

Blushing, Dash shrugged. "Glad to help," she told Berry.

"Berry, are you going to be all right walking?" Raina asked. "Maybe we should stop."

Slowly Berry stood up. "I think I'll be fine," she said. "Let's just go slow. I don't want to get another cut."

"Let's set up camp here," Raina suggested, looking around. "This is a nice flat surface. We've had a long journey, and we should get rest for tomorrow."

No one argued with Raina. After Berry's injury, they were all ready for a rest. They popped open their tent and spread out their blankets. If they were anywhere else, this might have been a fun campout, but they were all very aware of where they were sleeping . . . and thoughts of the goblins of Candy Cove filled their heads as they tried to get some rest.

CHAPTER 9

Black Licorice Night

"Did you hear that?" Cocoa asked. She pulled her blanket up to her chin. She had not been able to fall asleep. She wasn't sure what—or who—was making that noise outside the tent.

"That's a chocolate owl," Raina said, rolling over. "They can hoot all night. Let's try to get some sleep."

"That was *not* a chocolate owl," Cocoa said. Her eyes were wide open as she scanned the tent. She moved closer to Raina. "How can you sleep through this?" She pulled the blanket away from Raina's face. "Are you really sleeping?"

Raina opened one eye. "Not anymore," she groaned. She put her pillow over her head. "Go to sleep!"

Melli sat up. "I heard something too," she said, looking over at Cocoa.

"Me three," Dash chimed in. "It sounds like someone is scurrying around out there."

Berry sat up and snapped open a peppermint. "This is a little scary," she admitted. "Anyone else having a hard time sleeping?"

Cocoa, Melli, and Dash nodded. They looked over at Raina, waiting to hear her reply.

The tired Gummy Fairy threw off her pillow and blanket. "Well, I was trying to get some rest," Raina said. "But that sound is keeping me up. And now you are too!"

"Ah, so you are awake!" Cocoa exclaimed. She threw her pillow gently at Raina. "And chocolate owls hoot, not howl."

"Well, does one of you want to walk around outside and see what is making that noise?" Raina asked.

 85

"Um, not really. It's darker than black licorice!" Dash replied quickly.

The five fairies looked at one another for a long moment.

Berry stood up. Maybe the darkness gave her courage she hadn't expected, but she volunteered to go out first.

"Don't forget the royal candy basket," Raina instructed. "That candy has come in handy so far."

"Maybe it was just the wind rustling against the tent," Dash said, trying to be helpful.

"Not likely," Berry told her. She took a step out of the tent. She waited for her eyes to adjust to the darkness. "It is very dark tonight. I can't see a thing."

"Not even a goblin?" Cocoa asked.

"Not even my hand in front of my face!" Berry replied.

Melli squeezed Cocoa's hand. "If there is a goblin," she said, "what will we say to him?"

"Hello?" Dash joked.

"Seriously," Cocoa said. "Do we have a plan?"

Berry climbed back inside the tent to face her friends. "We don't even know if there really are goblins. Let's see what's happening outside. So far I think our imaginations are scaring us more than anything."

"She's right," Raina said. "Let's just see what's out there."

Cocoa grabbed Melli's hand. She thought her friend would like holding hands—and she was feeling a little too nervous not to hold on to someone!

 87

"Dash, any more peppermints?" Berry asked.

"Never leave home without a supply," Dash said, grinning. She handed her friends more peppermints to light their way in the darkness.

Berry pulled open the tent flap and held out her peppermint. The soft green glow lit up the area, and she slowly stepped out.

Melli's fingers tightened around Cocoa's hand. Dash reached out to hold Raina's.

"I don't believe it," Berry said. She jumped back inside the tent, holding the flap of the tent closed. Her sudden move made the fairies all bump into one another and fall down in a heap.

"What?" her friends cried out together.

"Did you see goblins?" Melli asked. Her heart was racing. They didn't even have a plan!

The Fruit Fairy laughed. "No," she said. "It's

a family of black licorice bats! They have been flapping around and hitting the tent."

"Bats?" Dash asked. "What can we do about that?"

Reaching down for the royal candy basket, Berry stuck her hand in and took out the heart-shaped fruit chew. "I guess it's my turn to work some candy magic," she said with a smile. "There's nothing a black licorice bat likes more than a fruit chew. I'll make more, and I bet it will quiet them down. Then we can get some rest."

"Good thinking," Raina said. "But be careful. I don't really trust those bats. They are sneaky creatures."

"I'll be all right," Berry said bravely. "I know they'll be happy to see these treats. And maybe I can get some information from them."

"Not likely," Dash said. "Bats are kind of flippy."

Berry took the fruit chews outside the tent and put the candy down on a nearby rock. In seconds the whole family of bats flew down to eat.

Dash stuck her head out of the tent. "How's it going?" she asked nervously.

"Come on out," Berry said. "You have to check out the sky. The stars are incredible here. I can see the Milky Way!"

The four fairies slowly crept out of the safety of their tent. The cool breeze blew their wings, but there was a stillness now that the bats were eating. Raina looked up at the black sky.

"*Sweet,*" she gasped. "I have never seen so many stars."

"Don't they look like jewels?" Berry said.

"Now that I am out here, I am not scared anymore."

Cocoa sighed. "Maybe this place isn't so scary after all." She spun around. "I don't see a goblin or anything."

"Me neither," Melli said. She pointed up to the sky. "Hot caramel!" she cried. "I just saw a shooting star!"

"If I were a goblin," Dash said thoughtfully, "I would hang out here too. This place is amazing. I never knew there were that many stars in the night sky."

Berry leaned down and tried to get the bats to tell her about any goblins in the cove. Each bat shook its head. Though black licorice bats can't always be trusted, this time Berry believed them.

The five friends stargazed until their eyes were too heavy to stay open. At that moment the bats were peaceful and there was silence in the cove. With no goblins in sight, the fairies decided to go to sleep. They would have to continue their hunt tomorrow when they weren't so tired. Snuggled safely in their tent, the fairies drifted off to sleep, hoping that in the morning they would find the answer to this goblin story.

CHAPTER 10

Candy Clue

The next morning Melli stretched her arms and wings in the bright sunlight. Her friends were still asleep inside the tent, so she had slipped outside. She took a deep breath and enjoyed the sweet, cool air of Sugar Cove. The Candy Cliffs were glistening in the morning light, and a few vanilla seagulls were cawing in a nearby tree.

Melli smiled. She loved all the different sweet sounds and scents of the cove . . . especially now that the bright sun was out!

She flew up and looked down at the bright blue sea below. She could see the caramel turtles crawling around the beach. When they weren't rocking the sailboat, the creatures were not scary at all. Melli took a quick dive and floated down to the beach.

No wonder this is called Sprinkle Sand Beach, she thought as she landed. In the evening when they had arrived, she hadn't noticed that the sand was actually made of rainbow sprinkles. She put her hand down on the sand and cupped the sprinkles in her palm. Opening her fist, she let the tiny, colorful grains fall through her fingers. Then she looked up to see a small turtle coming up to her.

Slowly reaching out her hand, Melli offered the turtle a caramel in the center of her palm. His shell had a beautiful mosaic, and he had the sweetest brown eyes.

"Hi there," Melli said. "I thought you'd like a little caramel for breakfast." She laughed as the turtle's soft tongue lapped up the candy. "Don't worry," she said to the others. "I made more. I have plenty more for all of you."

Soon the caramel turtles surrounded Melli. They waited patiently as she gave each of them a sweet morning treat.

"You weren't so nice to us in the sailboat last night," she scolded playfully. "I know you were probably scared." She leaned in closer to tell her secret. "I was scared too. Have you ever seen Nillie? I bet she is pretty salty."

Behind a rock Melli noticed a dark caramel turtle. He had his head and legs pulled deep inside his shell.

"Oh, I didn't mean to frighten you again," Melli said gently. She got up and walked over to him. "Come on out and try some more of this candy."

The turtle didn't budge from his shell.

Melli placed the caramel in front of the turtle. "I'll leave the caramel right here for you," she said. "When you are ready, you can come out and eat."

Melli saw the turtle's head slowly jut out of his shell. He sniffed at the candy and snapped a bite.

"Sure as sugar," Melli said, smiling, "we are going to be friends."

"Sweet sugar!" Cocoa cried from above. "There you are."

Looking up, Melli spotted her four friends.

"We've been looking all over for you!" Berry said.

Raina landed next to Melli. "I knew you'd come back to see the turtles," she said, smiling. "They are supersweet."

"You've made a few new friends," Dash commented. She nodded to the many happy turtles surrounding Melli.

Melli pet the shy turtle next to her. "I've never seen anything like them," she said. "And to think that we were scared of them yesterday!"

"They are cute," Cocoa said, leaning down to

pet one on the head. "And I bet they are loving the attention from a Caramel Fairy."

"You've been feeding them, haven't you?" Dash asked.

Melli grinned. "I couldn't help but give them more caramel," she confessed. "They were hungry." She grinned at the shy turtle. "And they are so cute!"

Dash flew around the turtles, and they playfully snapped at her. "They are so funny," she said, laughing. "They are *so mint*!"

For the first time since they'd arrived, the friends all laughed.

"Look over there," Cocoa said. Her laughter stopped and her face had a serious, worried expression. "Hot chocolate, do you see that?"

The fairies stared at a trail of melted candy

that circled around a piece of red rock candy. The sprinkle sand looked as if it had been torched with fire.

"Oh, what a gooey mess," Dash gasped.

"Just like in Gummy Forest," Raina added. "This is a clue. We have to follow the trail. This trail has to take us closer to the goblins." She glanced at her friends. "Or whatever is melting the candy."

The fairies all nodded at the same time. While they were having fun, they knew that this was not just a camping vacation. They had a responsibility to find the goblins of Sugar Cove.

"I think we have to follow the clue," Cocoa finally said.

"Where there's melted candy, there has to be fire," Berry said bravely.

101

"Or angry goblins?" Dash mumbled.

Raina led the way. "Let's stick together," she said. "We're on the right track. We have to get to the bottom of this mystery."

CHAPTER
11

Red Hot Idea

In a single line the fairies flew over the gooey trail. The melted sugar path snaked around the mountain and up into the Candy Cliffs. The path seemed to wrap around and around . . . endlessly.

Where is this trail taking us? Raina wondered. She wasn't scared. She was curious. And the more curious she became, the braver she felt. They were so close to finding the answer to this melted mess mystery. Finally she would know what had caused the damage in Gummy Forest. She flew a little faster up the cliffs.

Squinting, she looked up. Then she glanced behind her to Berry. "Do you have your binoculars with you?" she asked.

Berry flew closer to Raina and reached into her bag. She handed the jeweled binoculars to Raina. "Here you go," she told her.

Raina fluttered to a stop and hovered in the air. She peered through the lenses to see up the cliffs.

"How far do you think this trail goes?" Berry asked. Her wings were getting tired. Flying up the side of the cliffs with the sea wind blowing was very difficult.

 104

"My guess is that this goes to that cave over there," Raina said, pointing to a cave high up on a cliff. She handed the binoculars back to Berry. "What do you think?"

"I think you're right," Berry said, looking through the binoculars.

"I hope so," Cocoa said, coming up behind Berry. "This is hard work."

"And I'm getting hungry," Dash grumbled as she stopped next to her friends.

Melli was at the end of the line and slowed down to float in the air with her friends. "Anyone else a little nervous?" she asked. Even though the sun was out and there was nothing to make her afraid, she wasn't sure what would happen when they got to the cave.

The five fairies knew this was the big moment

in their journey. No one said anything for a minute.

"We'll be okay," Raina finally said. "Come on, let's go see what's up there. We've come this far—now let's find out if there are goblins or not."

The fairies continued to follow the trail of melted candies and ended up at one of the high caves nestled in a cliff.

Suddenly Raina put her hand out, and the fairies all stopped.

"What?" Cocoa asked, flapping her wings. "What did you see?"

"I just heard something," Raina whispered.

"I heard that too," Berry said, looking at Raina.

Floating in the air, the fairies listened. The cool sea air carried a soft, faint moaning.

 106

With wide eyes, Dash shook her head. "Oh, I heard that," she whispered.

The moaning sound came again. It was more sad than scary, but the noise still made Melli shiver.

"That must be the goblins!" Melli cried.

Raina put her hand on her friend's arm. "We don't know anything for sure," she said. "We need to take a look." She gazed at her friends. "Everyone ready?"

"Let's go," Cocoa said. "The suspense is making me crazy."

"Candy crazy," Dash agreed. "Let's go."

The fairies continued to fly to the highest cave. This time they flew a little closer together.

There was a large pink chunk of rock candy jutting out of the mountain a little above the cave.

Raina landed on it first, and the others followed. They took a moment to rest their wings and catch their breath.

"Did you see that?" Raina asked in a hushed tone.

"See what?" Dash asked, looking around.

"Coming out from the cave," Raina whispered. "I saw a long tail . . ."

"A dragon's tail," Berry finished for her. "I saw it too! The tail sticking out of the cave was lime green with blue spots."

Cocoa's eyes bulged open. "Hot chocolate!" she shouted.

"Shhhh," her friends all shushed her.

Cocoa's hand flew up to her mouth. "Sorry," she whispered.

"You mean the trail leads to a dragon's lair?"

Melli asked. Her wings began to flutter as she grew more nervous.

"I hope it's not a dragon that likes to eat Candy Fairies," Dash said, feeling a little more worried than scared at the news.

Raina threw off her backpack and took out the Fairy Code Book. "I know that I've heard of a dragon with those colors," she mumbled to herself.

"You actually brought the Fairy Code Book?" Berry said, rolling her eyes.

Opening the book, Raina turned to a page with a picture of a dragon. She nodded. "And aren't you glad I did?" she said quietly. She pointed to an illustration of a green-and-purple dragon with blue spots.

Her friends gathered closely around as they

looked at the picture and information about a green-and-purple dragon with blue spots. "The dragon's name is Carobee," Raina read out loud. "He is known for blowing hot air."

"That would explain the melted candy!" Cocoa exclaimed.

Berry pointed to the Fairy Code Book. "That's no gooey goblin," she stated. "He's a dragon from Meringue Island!"

"Maybe he's lost?" Raina said sadly.

"Or maybe he's just hungry," Dash said, shuddering.

"I liked this better when we thought there were little, pesky goblins," Melli mumbled. "Dragons are dangerous!"

"What should we do?" Cocoa said. "I thought you're never supposed to wake a sleeping dragon."

"Not unless you have some food," Berry said, smiling. She held up the royal basket of candy. "This basket hasn't failed us yet."

"Let's hope he likes candy better than fairies," Dash replied.

"Sure as sugar, this is one of the craziest things we've done," Melli said.

"Think of Gummy Forest and that trail of gooey candy," Raina said to her. "We have to find the reason this is happening."

 111

"We'll all stick together," Cocoa said. "We can do this!"

They held hands and jumped down to the rock below to get a better look inside the cave.

Even asleep, the dragon's breath was hot and fiery.

"He could roast a marshmallow with that breath!" Dash whispered.

"He doesn't look so scary," Berry noted. The cave was dark, but the dragon was curled up like a sleeping baby. He had long eyelashes that hung down from his closed eyelids as he slept peacefully.

"He actually looks kinda . . . sweet," Raina replied.

"He's sleeping," Dash reminded her friends. "Everyone looks calm and sweet when sleeping."

"What candy do we have left?" Melli asked, looking in the basket. If Carobee suddenly woke up, she wanted to have the treat ready.

"There's some chocolate," Cocoa said. "I could make some chocolate for our toasty friend."

"I think that would be a red-hot idea," Raina said. "We'll wait until Carobee wakes up, then give him the treat."

"After some of my chocolate, we'll be fast friends," Cocoa assured her friends. "I can make the best chocolate."

"Can you make it extra sweet?" Melli asked. "Maybe that will help sweeten him up?"

Cocoa smiled. "I'll try," she said.

Now all they had to do was wait for the sleeping dragon to wake up.

CHAPTER

12

Goblin Chase

So this is goblin hunting?" Melli said, staring up at the bright blue sky. "I kind of imagined a goblin chase a little differently."

Berry laughed. "Something darker, with a little more hiding?" she said, giggling.

The fairies were lying down on the pink rock above Carobee's cave. They were all on their stomachs leaning over the edge, watching the sleeping dragon below. Carobee had not moved once all day. He was still sound asleep. His steamy hot breath was making a puddle of liquid sugar out of the rock-candy pillow he was sleeping on.

"At least we're waiting in the daylight," Cocoa added. "The views here are *choc-o-rific*!" she exclaimed. She gazed out into the vast Vanilla Sea. "I like Sugar Cove much better in the daytime."

"Can you imagine if there was snow here?" Dash said, checking out the steep incline of the cliffs. "If there were trails here like on the Frosted Mountains, I would sled so fast . . . *so mint*!"

"Well, things might change once Carobee wakes up," Melli said, peering down at the dragon's long tail.

"Why would he ever want to leave Meringue Island?" Berry wondered out loud. She looked out toward Meringue Island. The small island had many meringue peaks, and the majestic Meringue Mountains looked delicious. "If I lived there," Berry said wistfully, "I would never leave." Berry had only met one fairy from the island. Her name was Fruli. At first Berry had been very jealous of her because of her beautiful clothing, but they had become fast friends.

"Maybe Carobee isn't really into clothes," Dash said, tossing a small candy rock in the air and catching it in her mouth. "I don't really see him as having the greatest sense of fashion. I think his passion is fire—and sleeping."

"I guess if you are out breathing fire all night, it makes you sleep all day," Cocoa said, lying

117

down. "Licking lollipops," she sighed. "All this waiting is exhausting."

"Does the Fairy Code Book say anything more about Carobee?" Melli asked Raina.

Raina shook her head. "There are fairy tales about the dragon, but no real, helpful information," she said. "He doesn't seem to be salty, though." She paused and sat up on her knees. "I just wonder why he would go around melting candy. That is the real mystery."

"I think you might have a chance to ask him," Melli said. She pointed down below. The large, long dragon tail was lashing around.

"He's awake!" Dash exclaimed. "Is the chocolate ready?"

"Best chocolate ever created," Cocoa boasted. She held up the chocolate bar.

The fairies all looked at one another. This was the moment they had been waiting for all day.

"On the count of three," Raina instructed. "One . . . two . . . three."

The fairies all held hands and flew down below to hover just slightly above the dragon's lair. Cocoa held the special chocolate in her hand, ready to offer the treat to the dragon.

Carobee's large eyes were open, and opened even wider when the fairies came into his view. The dragon's nose twitched. One of his dark eyes locked on the chocolate. A roar came from the dragon's wide, long mouth. The fairies quaked and quivered when they saw all of Carobee's sharp teeth and felt the hot breath bursting forward. Luckily, the fairies were fast and sped out of the way of danger.

Cocoa dropped the chocolate on the ground before flying away and watched as the dragon lapped up the candy.

"Mmmm," the dragon moaned. "Thank you."

The polite response stunned the fairies.

"Did he just say 'thank you'?" Dash whispered.

"I did," Carobee said. "Thank you for that chocolate. The candy was very good."

The fairies all shared a surprised look. Now they were even more confused. A polite dragon? Now, why would a polite dragon be melting candy throughout Sugar Valley?

"Is your name Carobee?" Cocoa bravely asked.

Carobee nodded his large head. "How did you know?" he said.

120

"Raina practically memorized the Fairy Code Book," Dash blurted out, pointing to the Gummy Fairy. "And she carries the book everywhere."

"Dash!" Raina exclaimed, very embarrassed. "I don't think that Carobee wants to hear all about *that*."

Sitting up, Carobee nodded again. "I do," he said. "You mean I'm in your book? What does the book say about me?"

Raina blushed. "Not much, unfortunately," she said.

Carobee swung his tail around to make room for the fairies. "How did you find me here?" he asked.

The fairies all shared a look again. This was not the greeting they had expected!

 121

"Well," Berry said, "we followed the melted candy trail."

"There have been lots of reports of melted sugar around Sugar Valley," Raina added. "And the trail from Sprinkle Sands Beach led us here to the Candy Cliffs."

"We thought goblins were haunting Sugar Valley," Dash explained.

"Goblins?" Carobee said. He hung his head. "Oh, fierce fires," he said, sighing. "I didn't mean to make such a mess."

"It would be hard to miss the gooey mess," Dash said. Then her hand flew up to her mouth. Sometimes her minty nature caused her to say things without thinking first! The dragon had the saddest look in his eyes. Dash felt terrible for her comment.

Melli flew closer to the gentle dragon. "Are you looking for something?"

There was a long pause. The fairies weren't sure what Carobee would say. Finally the dragon lifted his head.

"I'm lost," he said. "I am from the Meringue Mountains, and I can't seem to find my cave. This is the closest place I've found, but it's still not home. And I can't seem to make my candy here. I didn't mean to melt the candy in your Sugar Valley."

The fairies suddenly understood. There were no mean, scary goblins. Here was a scared, lost creature . . . and they all wanted to help.

13

Sweet Help

The fairies settled in closer to the friendly, sweet dragon.

"I wasn't sure where I was the other day," he explained. "The candy looked very different from home. There were no mounds of sugar on the shore."

Raina tapped her finger to her chin. This was all making sense to her. Carobee had landed on the shores of Gummy Forest and Black Licorice Swamp by mistake. Those places had different candy crops than the dragon's homeland. The shores of Meringue Island were known for mounds of soft white sugar along the shore. The fairies there whipped the sugar to make meringue with special wands. If Raina's hunch was right, plain sugar was what Carobee was searching for to make his candy.

"But Meringue Island is right over there," Dash said. She stood up and pointed out to the Vanilla Sea. When she did, she realized that there was still a heavy haze on the horizon and she couldn't see the island. "Well, it was there," she said, confused.

"We could barely see Meringue Island when we were in the sailboat," Berry added.

"This is the first time I've been away from home," Carobee said. He flopped his head down on his front legs. "And now I can't find my way back. Even Nillie tried to help me, but she couldn't."

Melli's wings froze. "Did you just say 'Nillie'?" she gasped.

"Yes," Carobee replied. "She tried to help, but she couldn't see through the fog either."

"We can help you," Cocoa said, full of confidence.

"Wait," Melli said, holding up her hand. "Did everyone hear Carobee mention Nillie?"

Carobee lifted his head. "Do you know Nillie?" he asked.

"Oh, no," Dash said, shaking her head. "And we don't want to meet her anytime soon."

Berry jumped up. "You shouldn't say that," she snapped. "Nillie tried to help Carobee, so she can't be all that sour."

"She's not sour at all," Carobee said. "She's a sweetheart."

"For real?" Melli asked, her brown eyes wide.

"Yes," Raina said. "You see? You can't believe all those tall tales you hear from the fairies." She turned to Carobee. "We have a map and a compass, and we can get you safely home."

The dragon flapped his tail to the side. "I wouldn't be able to fit on a fairy boat," he said. "It's no use."

The fairies all looked to Raina. She smiled. "We could ride on your back, Carobee. With us helping you, you'll be home in a peppermint flash."

Dash clapped her hands. "What a great idea!" she exclaimed. "How fast can you fly?" Once again Dash saw the looks on her friends' faces. "Sorry," she mumbled. "I just have never flown on a dragon's back before."

Carobee put his head back down on the ground. "Well, unless I can find something to eat, I won't be doing any flying. I don't have enough energy to fly anymore."

"Oh, that's sour," Berry said. "Maybe there's something we can do." She looked over at the princess's candy basket. The basket seemed a little too small to hold anything large enough to fill a dragon's stomach.

"What kind of candy do you make?" Dash

asked. "We're all Candy Fairies, you know."

"Carobee needs plain sugar," Raina said.

"Yes," Carobee said. "This rock candy doesn't work. And no place that I've been to has the same sugar as home."

The fairy friends all shared a worried look. They knew what it felt like to be far from home and not have all the usual comforts. At least they had brought candy with them and had their own magic to create more.

"On Meringue Island there are mounds of sugar along the shoreline for dragons to blow on and whip up cotton candy," Raina explained to her friends.

"We don't have scary, mischievous goblins," Melli said. "We have a lost, hungry dragon."

Dash grinned. "We can help you with the

hungry part," she told Carobee. "I'm hungry all the time."

"Sure as sugar," Melli added.

All the fairies nodded enthusiastically.

Raina stood up and walked in front of Carobee. "I have a plan," she said happily. "A *sugar-tastic* cure for this gooey problem!"

For the first time Carobee's eyes were filled with hope. "Really?" he asked.

"Pure sugar," Raina told him. "I think we might have some plain sugar in the basket."

Melli searched the basket and pulled out a small sack of royal white sugar. She grinned as she held up the bag. Princess Lolli had given them a little extra—just in case. "I bet if we all concentrate, we can make more for Carobee," she said.

"Let's try," Berry said.

Raina dumped the sugar on the ground in front of Carobee. The fairies all held hands and closed their eyes. Each of them fluttered her wings and thought sweet thoughts. In seconds there was a large mound of sugar!

"Sweet sands!" Carobee exclaimed. "How did you do that?"

"A little sweetness," Raina said, "always helps." She smiled at her friends.

Carobee stood up. He stretched his wide lavender wings. "You'll need to stay back," he said.

The fairies flew back up to the rock above the cave. Then Carobee blew a stream of hot air, whipping the sugar into a circle. As the hot air moved the sugar around, the sugar started to look more like cotton candy, not plain sugar.

"You did it!" the fairies cried.

"I wouldn't have been able to do this without all of you," he said. "I never meant to melt your candy. My fire is supposed to be used to create candy, not melt candy." His long tongue reached

out for a gulp of cotton candy. "This is the best cotton candy I've ever had." He licked his lips.

"Can I try some?" Dash asked.

"Yes, please," Carobee said. "Take some! With each bite I taste slightly different flavors. There's a hint of rainbow, fruit, and caramel." He took another bite. "Even some chocolate and mint!"

The fairies all grinned as they feasted on the cotton candy with their new friend. Only Raina looked a little concerned. She hoped they would be able to find Meringue Island in the dense fog.

CHAPTER 14

Secret of the Sea

Berry saw Raina staring at the map and flew up behind her. "What are you doing?" she asked.

"I'm trying to chart out a path for us," she said. "I want to make sure Carobee gets home. He seems really homesick."

Over her shoulder Berry saw Carobee and Dash eating cotton candy. "He looks happier now," she commented. "I think he was just lonely."

"At least we all have one another," Raina said. "I'm glad we all came on this journey together."

"Sure as sugar!" Berry said. She put her arm around Raina. "Don't worry, we'll be able to guide him home."

"But we do have to fly over the Vanilla Sea," Raina said. "Even for a dragon Carobee's size that can be pretty sticky."

"We'll be all right," Berry assured her. "We've done a pretty sweet job so far."

"You can say that again!" Dash exclaimed. Her lips were stained with a rainbow of cotton candy. She flew closer to her friends. "Carobee's candy is the best!"

Melli stroked Carobee's long snout. "Are you ready to go home?" she asked.

"Only if you promise to come visit me," the dragon replied. "You are the sweetest friends I've ever had."

The fairies all smiled.

"Come on," Raina said, rolling up the map. "Let's get going. The winds don't seem so bad right now."

The fairies flew up to Carobee's back and grabbed hold of him.

"Wait!" Berry cried. "We have the black licorice rope that Mogu gave us in the royal candy basket. We can use that as rope to help steer Carobee."

"And to hold on," Raina added. She looked down. Carobee was very big when he stood up, and she was far from the ground.

"So mint!" Dash exclaimed. "We are going to soar over the sea!" She sat up straight and grabbed the licorice rope that Berry tossed her.

After Berry had tied the rope around Carobee, she checked to see if the dragon was feeling all right. "If we want you to go left, we'll tug gently that way." She motioned for Dash to pull the rope. "And if we want to go right, we'll pull the other way."

Carobee nodded. "Good plan," he said. "Everyone holding on?"

"We're ready," Melli said, though she didn't say how nervous she was about flying over the Vanilla Sea.

The dragon gave a roar and took a running leap. The five fairies all gasped as Carobee sailed

off the cliff. His wide lavender wings spread out, and he soared out into the sky above the Vanilla Sea. Dash held the licorice reins in her hands and followed the route that Raina had charted. Even though she couldn't see very clearly through the fog, she knew Raina's map charting and Berry's compass would keep them on course.

"Wow," Berry said, looking around. "This is higher than I've ever flown."

"This is *sugar-tacular*," Raina added. "Everything looks so small from up here."

Suddenly Carobee took a nosedive. He was speeding straight down to the sea!

Melli held on tightly to the slippery licorice rope. "Hot caramel!" she cried. "What is going on?"

Carobee turned his head. "I see Nillie down

there," he said. "I want you all to meet her."

"Meet Nillie?" Mellie gasped. "Are you nuts?"

Raina shot Melli a look. "If she is a friend of Carobee's, then she's bound to be a friend of ours."

Swooping down, Carobee landed smoothly on the sea's surface. The water was a little choppy so the fairies held on tightly.

"There she is!" Carobee shouted as he came to a stop.

The fairies all looked into the water.

Melli's mouth flew open.

Dash just pointed.

And Cocoa, Berry, and Raina were also speechless.

"She's no sea serpent!" Melli finally managed to say.

 141

Carobee laughed. "Is that why you were all afraid?" he asked. "You thought those fairy tales about Nillie were true?"

The five fairies all nodded . . . shamefully. In the water next to Carobee was a beautiful pink sea horse. She had a rainbow mane and long dark eyelashes surrounding her big sea-blue eyes.

"Hello," Nillie said.

"I'd like you to meet my friends," Carobee said to Nillie. "They are helping me find my home."

The lovely sea horse bowed her head. "A sweet pleasure," she said.

The fairies were all too shocked to say a word. A long moment passed before Raina spoke up. "I'm sorry," she said. "We're just so surprised to see you . . . um, I mean meet you."

 142

Nillie titled her head back and laughed. Her laughter was like a gentle wind. "I'm sure this is surprising to you," she said. "I've long been a secret of the sea. Ever since I started to rule the Vanilla Sea, I have found that creatures leave us alone here if fairy tales of a sea serpent are told. This keeps the turtles and other sea life safe."

The fairies were still silent. They were so taken with Nillie's beauty and gentle voice.

"I saw how you looked after the turtles," she said. "Thank you for your kindness."

"They were very sweet," Melli said softly. "It was our pleasure."

"I am sorry that you had a rocky start to your journey," Nillie said. "But I wasn't sure of you or what your plans were in the sea. There have been some greedy, salty trolls in the past. And sometimes even fairies seeking new candy." She looked over at Carobee. "But I see now that you were here to help."

"We're glad we got the real story," Raina told her. "There were many fairies in Sugar Valley who thought there was a goblin haunting Sugar Cove and the crops at home." She patted Carobee. "But now we understand that Carobee didn't mean any harm. He didn't mean to melt any candy crops. He was just lost and scared."

"Sure as sugar, he's no goblin!" Dash blurted out.

Nillie laughed. "No, Carobee is the sweetest," she said. Then her expression grew serious. "But now that you've learned my true identity, you must promise not to tell anyone."

The fairies all exchanged a look.

"Except please do tell Princess Lolli that I send my sweetest regards," the sea horse added with a smile. "I have long admired her."

"You and Princess Lolli know each other?" Melli asked.

"Of course," Berry said. "Princess Lolli knows everyone."

"And she is a true, pure friend," Nillie added. "Now I will send Sprinkle and Bean to fetch your sailboat. They will deliver the boat safely to the shores of Meringue Island and then guide you home. They know the sea better than anyone."

Sprinkle and Bean poked their heads through the water's surface. The two small sea horses were just as beautiful as Nillie.

"These are my twin babies," Nillie said. "You can trust them."

"Thank you," Raina said.

"Your secret is safe with us," Melli told her.

"Sure as sugar," Cocoa added.

Nillie smiled, nodded to Carobee, and dove back into the water. The five fairies all grinned at one another.

"Let's get Carobee home!" Dash said, taking the licorice reins in her hands.

"Sounds good to me!" Carobee said. He flapped his wide wings and set off toward Meringue Island.

CHAPTER
15

Home Sweet Home

Carobee's large wings spread open as the dragon flew through the fog. With the fairies guiding him with a compass, he was sure to find Meringue Island.

"Stay to the left," Raina advised. She kept checking the compass. "Good thing the *N* arrow is a bright lime green," she whispered to Berry.

"We wouldn't have been able to see it if the compass wasn't so bright!"

"This is *so mint*!" Dash exclaimed. She was loving the speed of this flight.

"Too bad you can't see," Carobee said. "The view is beautiful when there isn't so much fog."

"All I see is fog." Berry sighed. "I hope we can see a little of Meringue Island!"

"I see the beach!" Carobee shouted. He soared over the waves and right up onto the beach. His passengers all flew off and stood on the mounds of sugar.

Berry gasped. "Wow. This is unbelievable." She turned around and saw mounds of fine white sugar everywhere. With the clear blue Vanilla Sea lapping at the shore, it was one of the sweetest sights she had ever seen.

"Thank you," Carobee said. "I never would have gotten back home without you—and your compass."

Suddenly the fairies felt sad. They didn't want to say good-bye to their new friend. Each one flew up to Carobee's head and gave him a hug.

"Promise that one day you will come back and see me?" Carobee asked. "I would love to show you all the parts of the island." He turned to Berry. "And I could take you to the best clothes stores!"

Berry laughed. "You've got a deal," she said, grinning. "I'm glad we got you back home. Now you can make cotton candy again."

"And we don't have goblins in Sugar Valley!" Melli said, laughing.

 150

Just then Sprinkle and Bean surfaced near the shore with the sailboat in tow.

"I think that is our ride," Raina said. "Goodbye, Carobee. I hope to see you again soon."

"Yes," Carobee said. He turned his head, and a blast of hot air came out of his large mouth. When he faced the fairies again, he was holding a rainbow bouquet of cotton candy. "In each of your favorite flavors," he said. "Chocolate, fruit, rainbow, mint, and caramel."

The fairies were so touched . . . and happy! What a delicious gift! They each hugged Carobee again and took their treats back to the sailboat.

"We can swim with you most of the way," Bean said.

"But we'll have to leave you before you get to the Gummy Forest shore," Sprinkle added.

The fairies understood. They were happy to have the sea horses as their guides. The wind was still strong and the dense fog hanging low. The fog may not have lifted, but the fairies had solved the gooey goblin mystery.

With the wind in their sails and the twins guiding them, the trip home was quick. When Gummy Forest came into view, the fairies were both happy and sad.

 152

"Good-bye, Candy Fairies," Bean and Sprinkle said together.

"Thank you," the fairies replied.

"Please thank Nillie again for us," Melli said.

"We will!" they cried as they dove deep into the sea and swam safely home.

At the Gummy Forest dock, Princess Lolli was standing there to greet the fairies.

"Welcome home!" the beautiful princess exclaimed. "You've had quite an adventure." She helped each fairy off the boat.

"Thank you," Raina said. "We've had a big journey."

"There were no goblins in the cove," Dash reported. "It was Carobee, the cotton candy dragon!"

"Yes, I have heard," Princess Lolli said. "I

have also heard you were very kind to all the creatures you met." She smiled sweetly at them.

The fairies grinned with pride.

"The sugar flies were buzzing about your flight across the Vanilla Sea," the princess continued. "Everyone in Sugar Valley thanks you for your bravery."

"And we met Nillie," Melli blurted out. "The sea serpent says hello." She hoped Lolli knew who she meant.

"Ah, yes, I am glad to hear she is well!" Princess Lolli nodded. "She must have thought highly of all of you to appear before you. She is a special creature, and quite clever."

"Yes," Raina said, agreeing. "The stories of the sea serpent are spooky tales continued to

be spun by fairies to protect the animals of the Vanilla Sea."

"Yes," Princess Lolli said. "I am proud of you for being so understanding."

"We didn't find goblins," Dash said. "We met a friendly dragon . . . and a new friend."

"I'll take that any day," Melli said.

"And no more gooey candy!" Raina exclaimed.

Berry wrinkled her nose. "Licking lollipops, I won't miss that mess!"

"Sugar Valley is back to normal," Princess Lolli said, smiling.

Raina took a deep breath. "Ah, so nice to be home."

Melli looked at her friends. "Yes, and now there will be a fall harvest to pick!"

"Yum!" Dash shouted as she flew up in the sky. "And lots of candy to enjoy!"

The fairies all laughed and headed back home to their crops. The candy in Sugar Valley was perfectly sweet and safe once again.

The Sugar Ball

Cocoa smiled as she flew across Chocolate Woods. The sun was shining and the air was full of sweet, rich chocolate scents. The Chocolate Fairy spread her golden wings and glided down to Chocolate Falls. *Yum,* thought Cocoa as she licked her lips. There was nothing better than fresh milk chocolate.

"Cocoa!" Melli the Caramel Fairy called. "Over here!" Melli was sitting underneath a chocolate oak tree. She waved her hands to get Cocoa's attention.

Waving back, Cocoa fluttered down to her friend's side. Melli was always on time—or early. She was a shy fairy, but her sweet caramel nature was part of what kept their group of friends sticking together—no matter what.

"What a *choc-o-rific* day!" Cocoa sang. She smiled at her friend.

"Only one more week until the Sugar Ball," Melli burst out. "I can't wait!" She took out a light caramel twist from her bag. "What do you think? I just had to show you right away." She held up the long caramel rope candy for Cocoa to view.

"It looks delicious," Cocoa commented.

"Won't this be perfect for the sash on my dress?" Melli asked. "I've been searching for just the right size trim."

Cocoa laughed. All any of her friends could think about was the Sugar Ball at Candy Castle, and the dresses they'd wear to the party. The big summertime ball was the grandest—and sweetest—of the season. The Sugar Ball was a celebration of summer and the sugar harvest. Fairies from all over came to the Royal Gardens for the party. Princess Lolli, the ruling fairy princess, always made the party the most scrumptious of the year.

"I think that will be the perfect addition to your outfit," Cocoa said. She touched the golden caramel twist. "This is the exact right color for your dress."

Melli clapped her hands. "I knew you'd say that!" she said, grinning. "Cara wanted me to make her one just like this too."

Cara was Melli's little sister and always wanted to be just like her big sister.

"Did you help her?" Cocoa asked.

"Sure," Melli said. "She's so excited about her first ball." She stopped and admired her dress. "Now I just need to find the right necklace."

"You should ask Berry to make you one of her sparkly fruit-chew necklaces," Cocoa said. She was used to her friend Berry the Fruit Fairy always talking about fashion, but this year all her friends were concerned about their Sugar Ball dresses and jewelry. Everyone wanted to make her ball gown special and unique. Even Cocoa!

"You're right," Melli said. "I should ask Berry.

I just hope she doesn't say she's too busy. Did you know that she is weaving the material for her dress herself? Her dress is going to be *sweet-tacular*!"

"Hmm," Cocoa muttered. She was actually growing a little tired of all the talk about dresses. Even though she wanted to look her best, she had another idea of how to make her entrance at the ball special.